MY KITCHEN

Harlow Rockwell

Greenwillow Books, New York

Published by Greenwillow Books, A Division of William Morrow & Company, Inc., 105 Madison Avenue, New York, N.Y. 10016 Printed in the United States of America First Edition 10 9 8 7 6 5 4 3 2 1

Library of Congress Cataloging in Publication Data

Rockwell, Harlow. My kitchen. Summary: A child explains how his lunch is prepared in the kitchen.
[1. Luncheons—Fiction. 2. Cookery—Fiction. 3. Kitchens—Fiction] I. Title.
PZ7.R59485My [E] 79-15929 ISBN 0-688-80236-2 ISBN 0-688-84236-4 lib. bdg.

When I come home,

I go to my kitchen.

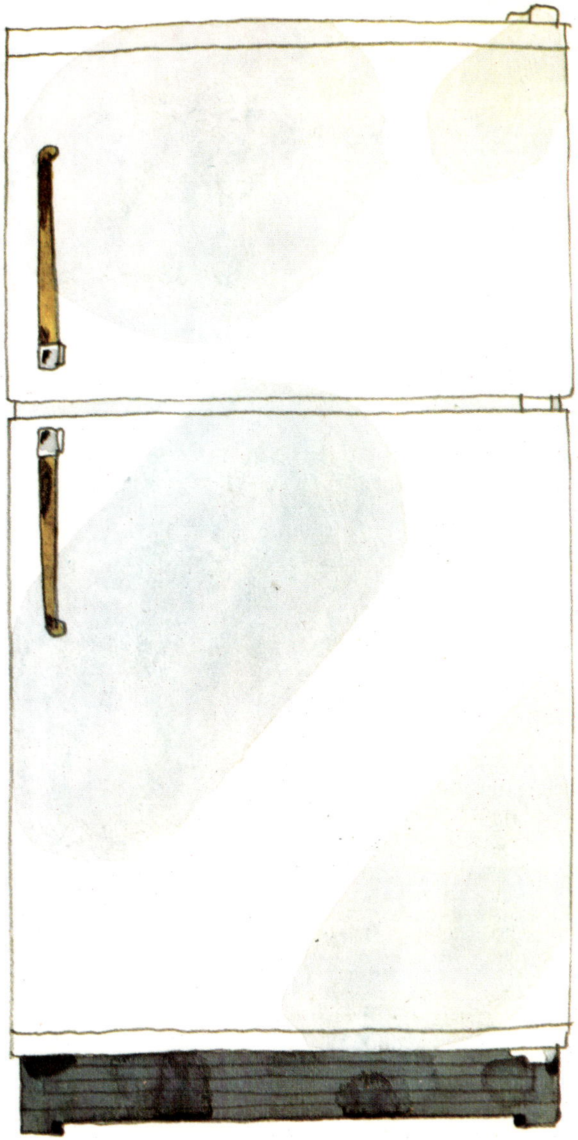

There is a refrigerator

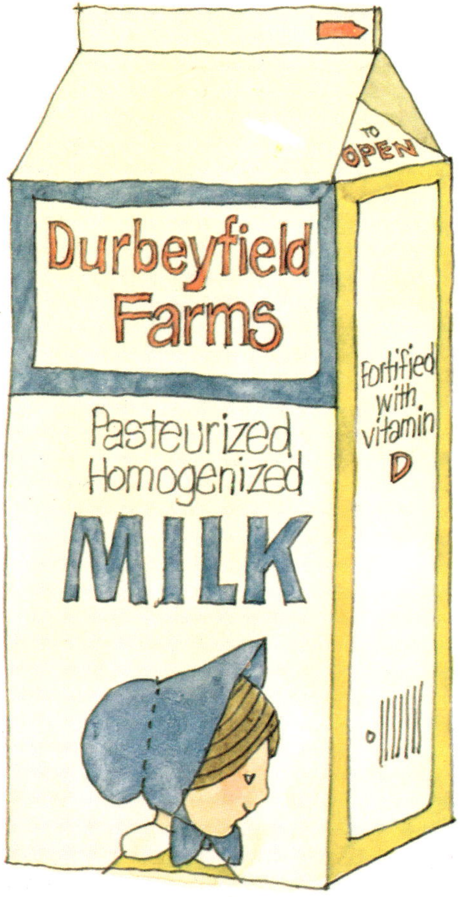

where they keep my milk.

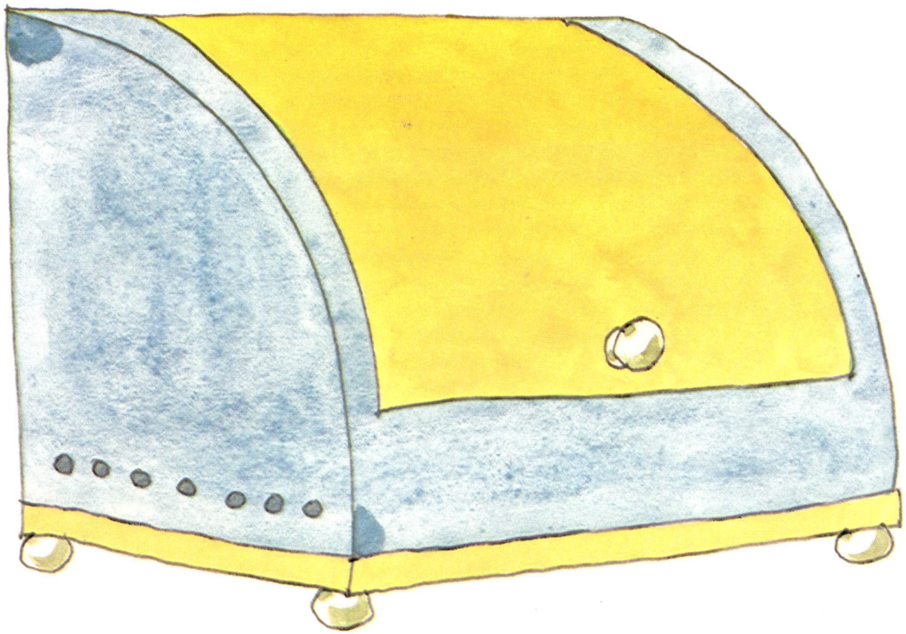

There is a bread box

where they keep my bread.

The peanut butter
is on the shelf.

So is the can of soup.

So many things

are on the shelf!

The spoon
comes out of the drawer

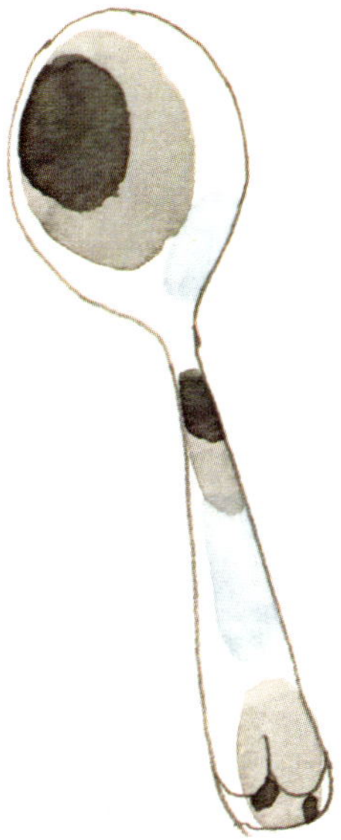

and is set upon the table.

The bowl and plate
come off the shelf,

and onto the table.

My favorite glass
was in the sink,

but now it is clean and on the table.

My napkin is on the table too.

The pots and pans
are in the cabinet.

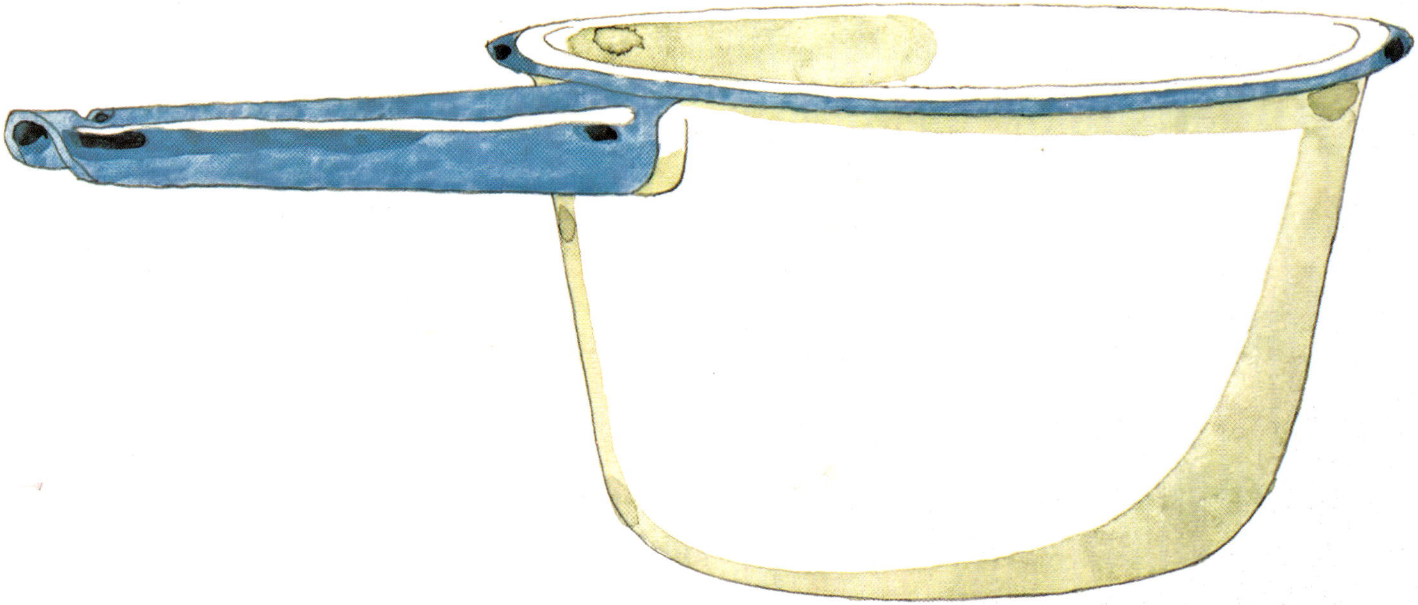

Here is the pot for soup.

The can opener opens the can.

The soup goes in the pot.

The pot goes on the stove.

The fire is hot.

The peanut butter
goes on the bread.

My soup is hot.
My milk is in my glass.
My sandwich is made.
My lunch is good!